The Book of Destiny

A Tale of Unanswered Questions

notionpress
.com

The Book of Destiny

A Tale of Unanswered Questions

ANKIT KAPOOR

notionpress.com

Notion Press

Old No. 38, New No. 6

McNichols Road, Chetpet

Chennai - 600 031

First Published by Notion Press 2015

ISBN: 978-93-5206-199-0

Acknowledgements

I would firstly like to thank my father, Mr. Ajay Kapoor, and my mother, Mrs. Jyoti Kapoor who have always motivated and encouraged me to write, even on the most stupid topics.

I would also like to thank my younger sister, Mannat Kapoor and my younger brother Vedant Kapoor, who sat with me all the time giving me some ideas even though they were mostly not of much use to me. Even when I thought that I was using some wrong vocabulary, those people would just shake their heads blankly, giving me more confidence that I am still going right…

A special thanks to my uncle, Mr. Rajat Kapoor, my aunt Mrs. Manisha Kapoor, my grandfather, Mr. A. C. Kapoor and my grandmother, Mrs. Madhu Kapoor. They were never on the forefront but helped solve all the backstage problems. All of them just happily clapped and whistled whenever I would present any of my poems or stories which gave me the confidence to keep going… I would also like to thank my other set of grandparents Mr. B.M.K

Chopra and Mrs. Rama Chopra for their constant encouragement and praise.

My sincere thanks to my classmates, my teachers and my Principal at Bhavans Civil Lines, Nagpur. All of them just admired my poems and kept on praising me.

Contents

Chapter 1

The Beginning

Hi friends! This is year 3012. I am around 1012 years old. This is obviously because I am immortal. Flummoxed? You think I am an idiot? Well, that thought is quite obvious. Anyone who appears before you randomly and says, "*Hey! I am a thousand years old!*" might seem like an idiot. Well, if you take it that way, then I suppose this story is idiotic, too!

Now, the Earth is not as simple and good as it was earlier. Now not only humans live here, but also robots and Martians, too. Around 2099, it was found that Mars was inhabited by living creatures. At that time, the Earth was as good as gone because of the increasing population and global warming. We went to Mars with a request to share the planet. But the Martians were not as humble and soft-hearted as we thought they were. Instead of peace, friendship and sharing, there was hatred, impatience and war. Many died. Both sides lost people in huge numbers. Both planets then stabilized an alliance and lived together in peace. That was a long time ago. It is history now.

Now, I will tell you what this story is about. I am Anay. This is the story of my life: how it began, how it unfolded, and how I died and all the revolutions that took place. Do you know the reason for all this? Obviously not! This was the outcome of the lives of six people – Anay (me), Sanya, Taman, Vensolio, Alkazar and Lavenred.

These were people. The most unbelievable part of the story is that this was all done for a book that had magical powers. I can probably read your mind now. You think I am an idiot. That's exactly how I feel when I think about my life. Frankly, I am not into deep spiritual thoughts and philosophy. But after this incident, I am convinced of one thing: whenever evil arises, it will take different forms. But to stop evil, good can come, through someone.

The chosen one would have to keep his secrets and pay the cost of doing so, too. But the chosen one would have to save people from evil. I was the Chosen One. We were all the Chosen Ones. We made sacrifices, some of which were painful. Now when I look at myself, I feel proud to be the Chosen One. This might seem to be philosophical now, but once you read my life, you will know what, how and why I feel what I feel.

Chapter 2

Lavenred

It was a peaceful evening. I was in the Seventh Grade then. Like most other students, I felt that education was boring. We sat in a closed room for around eight hours, to read books. It was nothing like what we do today, where we have audio-command text, voice-simulating books, and audio-auto-type tablets. Anyway, coming back to the story, it was a very tiring day. It was evening and I was back from school at around 4:00 PM. I threw my bag and removed my shoes and socks, and switched on the air conditioner. I sat on my couch, and began fidgeting with my phone.

"Mom, where's dad?" I asked, immersed in my phone.

It was a lame question to ask since most of the times, I would know where he was. He would either be busy at a meeting, or at a friend's party. Vijay was my dad. He was a good man, and a man who kept his commitments. He was a bit of an alcoholic, but would drink only at parties. He loved to party. That day, he was at a party.

"One drink, please! A red wine!" Dad said to the bartender. He was not interested in the party that day, maybe because he had been there for too long. He loved things that were short and fast. He was impatient, and not tolerant enough to drag something for long. He was a confident man, a person of remarkable chutzpah. Maybe he was intending to leave the party then.

"You are into drinks, aren't you?" a heavy voice came from behind him. He did not take a second to change his thoughts.

"Oh! Mr. Lavenred! What a pleasant surprise to see you here!" Dad said.

"Hello, Mr. Vijay. It's my pleasure."

The next fifteen minutes were spent on a formal handshake, a glass of wine each, and a "How are you? Very well, thank you." The next three hours saw personal conversations with smiles on both faces. For two more hours, there was laughter, and a strong friendship.

It was late when he was back from the party. He spoke about Lavenred. Lavenred and dad had turned from strangers to friends. It was a gradual process. They started meeting regularly, talking, having dinner and lunch together. They partied and planned holidays together. Soon, they became best friends. That was where it began. The first root had changed a seed into a healthy sprout. It was the starting point that signified the birth of a massive plant that would grow gradually.

It became a mundane affair to see Lavenred. Every day, he appeared out of the blue with a completely new reason. Whenever Lavenred came to our house, he would see me and give me a broad smile. I never liked the smile. I don't know why, but I never felt comfortable with Lavenred. I was always in deep thought about him. Though my father always trusted him, I found him untrustworthy. But how could I have stopped him from coming home? I was a child then! Time flew. It was now eight years since Lavenred and dad had become friends. Their friendship had become stronger than the best. Time had flown by and I didn't realize when I grew up. I turned from twelve to twenty.

In the meantime, dad expanded his business a lot too. He acquired many companies. Among them was a mining company, where he had a 50% partnership with someone called Sharma. The acquisition of this company was the second biggest mistake dad had made. The reason for my telling you about this company is briefly telling you how we got the Book of Destiny. The biggest story of the millennia was about to come into existence. Some pathetic mistakes were to be made. Powers beyond our reach were to be conquered. A revolution was going to set in. Lives were going to change. The story had to be started on a day not far away.

Chapter 3

A Strange Happening

A day that I wished should have never come had been standing on my dying hope. I was not eager or excited about that day. That morning, dad had gone to see some land for his mining business. Instead of 'a', I should actually be saying 'the', because the visit to the place was another biggest mistake that I should have prevented from happening. I was not able to because I was still asleep when dad left. The place was far away from the main city. It was like going to Australia by road, that too from India. But dad was habituated to such trips. It was a long ride but he finally reached the place.

I felt strange about the land being situated in a village. You might be wondering why that makes it strange. The village was a set for horror movies and was used to create fear and horror. The only difference was that the sets were created for a scene, but all this was original. The village did creep people out – it might have appeared normal to all appearances, but there was something creepy about it. It gave an impression of horror and anxiety. Though I respect my dad, I would like to say that he should have worked more on listening to his heart rather than his brain. But he was a businessman, so that would not have happened.

Ignoring the villagers, he went to the land. He saw that everyone was ready, and were waiting for him. The co-owner of dad's company, Mr. Sharma, was there. His presence there seemed like it was out of the blue because it was once in a blue moon that he appeared. Both dad and Mr. Sharma shook hands.

"Wow! What a wonderful place for people of our kind, right Vijay?" Sharma said as both of them climbed up to get a good view of the mine. It was huge, indeed. It also had a certain look about it that I remember till date. How can I forget it? That day changed our lives completely. The scorching heat and light of the sun no longer allowed them to stand in the mine. Both of them went to a van-like vehicle. They felt lazy there, so they came out in the sun to continue working. Soon, everyone was busy. Labourers dug into the mines and Sharma supervised them. Dad was discussing plans. Everything seemed normal until things suddenly changed. No one could have anticipated that something was going to go wrong, but you can't trust time. It can by your greatest friend and the worst enemy all at once. The digging stopped. In the first seven minutes, everyone thought it was a break. In the next three minutes, everyone understood it was not a break as a crowd started to build walls around the place. In the next one-and-a-half minutes, it was obvious that something fishy was going on. Every activity in the mine had stopped. In the next half minute, dad and Sharma came to see what was happening. These twelve minutes changed the chapter for history.

What everyone thought was a small penetrable sand bed, actually was a piece of impenetrable rock. This was quite unusual because even for a mine, to find hundred percent mineral rocks at such a small depth of a meter was unbelievable. Sharma was staring at it with his mouth open, his face a portrait of happiness. What he saw was money and profit. What dad saw was suspense and fishiness. Work had completely stopped. Everyone was surprised at what was happening. After a break, work resumed. The moment tools struck the rock, the clear sunny day turned into a stormy sky. The clouds had formed a very odd pattern. The workers lost their senses. The superstitious ones began to narrate tales of their great grandfathers' experiences of the same thing. Thinking that it might be a co-incidence, these people were sent back to work. Dad didn't think this was a natural accident, and began to take photos of the sky. As soon as he did that, the sun showed up once again.

Sharma was horrified by all this. He was a fairly superstitious and this scared him. He stopped coming to the mine after that day. Dad continued to visit the mine. For the next three days, there was nothing different. On the fourth day since the happening, there was something weird. When dad reached the place, the bed rock was almost gone. He got busy with his finances and the deals for the mine. Around half-an-hour later, work stopped again. A crowd appeared near the ground. Dad stood with them too. When the rock was shifted a titanium-coated square shaped rock was seen beneath it. When the workers tried to use electrical tools on it, the tools didn't work. It was found that the magnetic field was quiet unusual around the square. When the rock was lifted from above the titanium coated rock, they saw some moulds in which a strange liquid was found. The moment it came in contact with sunlight, it turned into gold of a hundred percent purity. Dad was confused. He noticed that the patterns formed by gold resembled the ones formed by the clouds in the sky. He clicked a pictured of the rock too. The experts were busy trying to find out what the liquid was. The workers, instead of working, were chatting in groups. Dad was lost in thought.

Dad came home early. He sat in his room, alone, not wanting to be disturbed by anyone. He gazed at the images of the rock and the sky in his camera. According to his study, he concluded that this was some kind of a dead language. That very moment, he called a language specialist home. They spent a great deal of time in his room. After two hours, the expert left. Dad was very disturbed. The thing on the clouds said this: "Beneath the ground lies the answer…", while the thing on the rock said this: "Beneath this rock lies the way to silver and gold. Whoever lets hands upon the wooden chest becomes God!"

Chapter 4

Dust a Book

That night, dad wasn't able to sleep. He was thinking about the messages on the rocks. Dad could have called the trouble off by not getting into it so deeply. I wish my dad was not so inquisitive about things. He called up Sharma.

"Come to the mine today. There's something I want to tell you!" he said. He was in such a hurry that he didn't listen to Sharma's reply. He reached the site in a few hours and waited for Sharma to arrive. The workers had been told not to work until further orders. Soon, Sharma arrived.

"What did you want to tell me so desperately?" Sharma said, as he got off the car. "It's even worse than what happened that day," Dad said.

They went to a cabin. The workers were ordered to start work. They had to lift the titanium coated stone. It was a heavy one, weighing over five tones. Dad told Sharma the complete story. The first thing

Sharma did after listening to the story was to control his laughter. He then started to get annoyed. After dad told him the story, he waited for Sharma to say something. Sharma was more annoyed.

"What a story! Vijay, I never knew you were into science fiction. What the hell do you think? That I am a fool? A treasure? A map? From sky? A chest of so-called secrets? This is all so jolly! I never expected such a thing from you, Vijay!" Sharma said, angrily.

"You don't believe me, do you? Then see this yourself," Dad said, controlling his anger.

They went to the mine. By the time they reached, the rock had almost been lifted. Sharma was astonished at the first look of the rock. He took off his goggles, and went ahead slowly with his mouth open in astonishment. He looked at dad and then looked down. It was not a time to smile, but dad giggled. Soon, the rock was lifted. Under it, there was a wooden box that was shining as though there was all gold and silver inside it. It was heavy, and there was something strange about the. It was locked with a lock made of stone, with some patterns on it. The patterns did not resemble those in the sky or the stone. Dad clicked pictures of it, too. People tried to break the lock, but it seemed invincible. Every tool and machine was tried on the lock for four hours. It had now grown dark. After hard work of four-and-a-half hours, the lock was broken.

Minutes before the lock was broken, everyone except for dad was excited.

"I bet it is some kind of great treasure!" Sharma said as he stood near dad.

"Well... according to its luster and weight, one can say that it is treasure but I don't feel that way. I feel that something is wrong," Dad said.

"Hey! Stop taking everything so seriously! This treasure can be helpful! Just imagine!" Sharma said as he went ahead.

The moment the lock was broken, there was lightning and thunder. A lightning bolt truck the box. It rose up into the air, and with a flash of light, the box fell to the ground. All the luster had disappeared, all its weight had gone. It had become a lifeless wooden chest. Dad and Sharma dismissed everyone from the site.

"So, let's open this thing," Sharma said. Dad opened the box, and they were surprised.

"What the... what the hell is this?" Sharma exclaimed. "A book? I am leaving this project! This has given me more loss than anything else in the ago. The man came back, overpowered the boy and took control over one of his friends. He sent the boy to another dimension, where he had sent many people. It seemed to be am impractical story. How can one be sure of another dimension? How can one capture another's mind? I was thinking about it when a voice floated into the room. "Anay come on! Lunch is ready," Taman said as he summoned me to the table. I went there. The table was arranged lavishly. I was hungry, and pounced on the table. Everyone was as hungry as I was. Alkazar just ate a spoon of curd, and while eating, spilt half of it on his shirt. Everyone started laughing. "Alkazar is surely back! You were right, Sanya!" said Vensolio. The laughter increased. It turned into a joyous lunch. Suddenly, I felt a sharp pain in my head. Laughter disappeared from my face. The pain increased. I held my head. Everyone's attention was on me. "I can't see clearly," I said. Everyone began shouting as I fell unconscious. I collapsed on my seat.

Chapter 20

Who Is It?

I was standing in a dark place. There was nothing. Suddenly, I heard a known voice.

"Hello, my boy!" it said. I couldn't see who it was. Only a dark, but well built and strong figure emerged. The face was still hidden in darkness.

"Who .... Who are you? What am I doing here? What is this place and what –"

"Just relax. Everything will be told to you, but at the right time. There is a chain of secrets you don't know." I was surprised. It was a known voice. I had heard this voice throughout my life, but I wasn't able to guess whose it was. I tried moving my hands. I couldn't feel them.

"Seriously man! This is the heights! Please tell me where I am! What the heck is going on? Where is the rest of my body?" I burst out in fear and anger.

"I said that answers will be reveled at the right..."

seemed old. I wondered how I hadn't read it at all. It had a loose binding and had worn out yellow pages. I lay on my bed and cracked the book open. I've always considered myself observant and prudent, but till date, I look back and wonder where my observation had gone that day. The moment I opened the book, I felt weird. The first page was empty. As I flipped through the pages, I saw that the whole book was empty. I was confused. How could such a thick book be empty? I had turned twenty-three, but I couldn't help thinking like a child. I thought that instead of keeping the book empty, I would write something in it. And so I did that. I picked up a pen, and started to scribble some random words. I don't remember what I thought, but I read out what I had written. I had written 'my woolen jacket changed to leather, and the sunny summer changes to rainy weather'. An extraordinary thing happened. What I had written began to disappear, letter by letter, word by word, line by line. Within moments of its disappearance, I saw something happening outside my window. I ran out to see the sun disappearing, and dark clouds taking over. It began raining. At the same time, I noticed that the blue jacket I had on me in wool, turned into black leather.

It felt like a dream. I instantly recollected what I had written, and I was shocked. It had all come true! I ran to my room and wrote in the book, 'there is a frog on my bed.' It was the most I could think of in my state of frenzied excitement. In minutes, the writing disappeared. The page looked like it had not been touched even once in a thousand years. I heard a croak and turned around to see a frog on my bed. This was not some ordinary book. My heart started pounding. I discovered an all new power! But what I didn't realize at that time was that there was something coming my way. This was short-lived excitement. Trouble of a very different kind, losses, grudges and adventure – were all going to start. The true power of The Book of Destiny would be revealed. The world's history was about to be re-written.

Chapter 6

The Real Meaning – A Forbidden Book

What was happening? How could it be? It defied every known rule of physics. But it was happening all the same, and I was sure that I was not dreaming. I waited for dad to come so I could tell him what all happened. Strangely, that day, dad was back home early. This was a once-in-a-blue-moon occurrence.

"How come you are back so early today, dad?" I asked.

"Today I have been invited by Lavenred. We will have dinner after a business meeting, and then I will go to his house. It'll be late. Take care of mom and sleep on time," Dad said.

What he said was his favorite dialogue, I heard him say it since I was twelve. By that time, I had forgotten about the book. Two hours later, I was on my bed and my room was locked. I examined the book, trying to find out what would happen next. Just then, I felt a chill down my spine. It made me uneasy. I felt cold. The next moment, my arms and legs were drained of all energy. I was left lying on the bed. I started feeling a vague numbness in my head. I was knocked out in a few seconds. In my mind's eye, I saw a brownish screen. A black silhouette was displayed on it. The figure seemed to look like dad. Gradually, another figure appeared. This resembled the profile of Lavenred. The next scene showed a fight between these two. Gradually, it turned into a battle. Both sides had extensive armies. The side opposite Lavenred was not lead by my dad – instead, five young people stood as leaders. The shadow showed four boys and a girl. The boy placed in the center looked like me! The scene gradually went blank. With a bright flash of light, The Book of Destiny appeared.

The screen gradually cleared up. Slowly, I regained my strength and worked up. It was so weird! I was confused. I didn't know what had happened. My mind was filled with questions. What was this? What could it have been? A dream? Maybe a thought? Or maybe it was more like a vision – an insight? Did it signify anything which was to happen? Something large? Something which could not be ignored? What relation did it have with the book? Why me? Was it planned somewhere that it was me who would have seen a vision? Why not mom or dad, perhaps? Was I the chosen one? Who were those four people with me? Whom were we fighting? What was this all for? Did the book have a reason for its existence? What was all of this? Was all this connected to the dinner that dad was about to have, with Lavenred?

I was lost in thought. I was in my room, so nobody saw me falling and there was no chaos. I was still recovering from the shock, when I heard a loud thumping sound. I went out of the room to see mom standing, stunned by what she saw. It was dad. He was red with anger. He was a short tempered man, but this rage was too much, even for him. We helped him in. I gave him a glass of cold water as he sat in his room. In a low voice, he was repeating something constantly. He probably didn't want anyone to listen to what he was speaking, but I heard it: "I have made a huge mistake."

I could connect the dots now. Something had happened between Lavenred and dad. I knew what it was but kept quiet. Mom had probably estimated what the issue was. So much happened that night that I forgot to tell dad about the book. It slipped my mind. But it was for the good, all the same. Had I told him about the book, he would have lost his temper and would have done something wrong. The next morning would be a better time to talk, I thought, and slept. The next day was a holiday. Dad was home. He seemed to have made peace with the chaotic mishap from the previous evening and seemed normal. By eleven in the morning, breakfast was done. Soon after, mom and dad went to their room. I went to mine. I was lounged on my bed and looked at my bookshelf, searching for a book to read. I realized I had to tell dad about The Book of Destiny, and rushed to his room with the book in tow. He was reading a book called "The end of the world." I sat on the bed.

"Dad, I guess you should see this," I said.

"Show it to me later. I am reading now," Dad replied, his eyes unmoving from his book.

"It's more important than science fiction," I said, firmly. "Son, what I am reading is more important than just another conspiracy theory that you are about to share with me," he said, with his eyes stuck on the book. Being the son of a short-tempered man, I inherited impatience. I started feeling agitated. "See it for yourself then," I said. I took the book and wrote in it: "Dad's book is torn into two pieces." Within moments after I read it out loud, his book was torn up. Dad looked up in astonishment. "You tore my book?" he exclaimed.

I smiled disarmingly. "A seven hundred page book, dad. And my biceps are not so strong either!" I said. "Then how....?" Dad asked, astonished. "This is what I wanted to show you!" I said, "And you saw it for yourself.

"What rubbish is this!?"

"Is it?"

"Yes, of course!"

"Want to see another example?" I wrote on the book: "Dad's white T shirt turns black." The words disappeared and his T-shirt turned black. Mom looked she was so surprised and could not find words to express what she wanted to say. It was a short lived astonishment for dad, as he suddenly frowned. "What happened?" I asked.

"Can... can this book complete any order written in it?"

"Yes. Yes it can!"

"Can it be used to serve a long-term purpose?"

"Yes. It actually can—"

"This is not happening. It is all connected. All the patterns on the stone and in the sky I had seen that day – they meant this book! 'The answer lies in the book', 'the one who has it becomes God', 'can control life'? The one who has the control of the book is God! Can you imagine what would happen if it falls into the wrong hands!? Nobody will touch this book. Give it to me. The use of this book is forbidden!" dad said. His face was white with fear. The book was locked in a safe, never to be touched again. Since then, it became the Forbidden Book.

Chapter 7

The Book Re-opened

It had been two years since the book was opened. It was now 2025. It was a case of 'out of sight out of mind' for me. We had forgotten about the book, until one day. It was a normal day, I remember it was May. It would have been one thirty or two when I left to a friend's house. It was about seven of evening when I was back home. When I entered the hall at home, I saw both mom and dad sitting in fear with their head in their hands. They seemed scared rather than sad. Dad was angry.

"What has happened? Why is the house in a mess?" I asked. Nobody answered. I caught a glimpse of dad's room. The light was flickering. I took a closer look. The cupboard was open, drawers were thrown across the room, clothes were all over the floor, curtains were torn, mattresses were thrown and the bed was displaced. I went into the dressing room, and opened the cupboard. A locker was partially opened. Surprisingly enough, the money and jewels were safe. I went out and told dad, "The money and jewels are safe? What has been stolen?" I choked before completing the sentence. A possibility dawned upon me. I went back to the room and opened another locker. My heart skipped a beat after looking at it: the locker with the book was broken into, and the book was gone.

A note Remained in place, saying: "I have it. Come and take it if you are a real man!" It was signed by Lavenred. The note fell from my hand. I could not think. Anxiety and fear had gotten the better of me. I was sweating with fear now. I ran out.

"When did this happen?" I asked.

"Fifteen minutes ago, your mom and I were home from our friend's house. We saw this when we were got home," dad said softly. Fear sucked all strength from him.

"There is no other way now. Let's stop Lavenred!" I said as I walked towards the door. We sat in the car, and drove to Lavenred's place. We entered his house. "Stop this stupidity Lavenred!" Dad screamed with mixed emotion.

"Why? Are you afraid of being a prisoner?" The deep and heavy voice of Lavenred sounded out.

"You swine!" dad couldn't control himself and punched Lavenred. As he fell, the book fell away to his hands.

"Anay! Take the book and tear the page!" dad said. I rushed to the book and found the page on which he had written. I was just about to tear it when I read it. My heart just stopped beating after reading what was written.

"In 2025, I am ruling the world. Anay, his family and all others like him are my prisoners. I am the ruler of the world and I am the most powerful man!"

"Anay, what is wrong with you?" Dad screamed. By the time I could do something, Lavenred took the book from me and started reading it aloud. Dad was almost unconscious, I couldn't do anything because of the shock.

"What do you think of the gutters, Vijay? Because in my reign, you are staying there!" he said.

Dad came to in sometime, and said "Anay, your mom!" I realized what he wanted to say and we ran back to the car. We sat in the car and went back to mom. When we got home, we saw mom at the doorstep. The house had disappeared. The empire had been set up. Evil had won over good.

Chapter 8

The Evil Empire – A Future Sight

Everything had changed. We were once rich, and dad was the director of many companies, but now, we were rotting in prison. Sharma was missing. We didn't know if he was alive, even. The city's Parliament House had become a part of Lavenred's home. The roads were occupied by guards. Gardens were taken over by big machines digging up the earth. He was trying to find crude oil in India. The remaining gardens became execution grounds. Buildings with many flats became prisons. The prison we were in was the closest to the parliament house. The other buildings were used as quarters for his servants. The city that once thrived with colours, was now dull. Gardens that once echoed with the sounds of children playing were now silent. Roads which were once crowded with traffic were empty. I was often annoyed by the noise and crowd of an urban life, but now, the silence was awful. It struck me why the adjective deadly is used with silence. The city had died. The world was dead silent. There was one ruler and the rest were slaves. The ruler was filled with cruelty, hatred, evilness and brutality. I was with my family, but, I still felt lonely. Suddenly, a chill shot up my spine. I was restless. I could see something in my dream. It was a vision, again. I saw three shadows. One was a man, the other a woman, and the third was a boy. I saw the head of the man being cut. I saw the lady being killed, and the same shadow had killed the both of them. The shadow looked similar to the one in the last vision. The boy was left alone. Some light came on the boy: he looked like me. The light faded and I saw the book again. What was it? Who was that shadow? Why were the man and woman killed? Who killed him? Why did he kill them? Who was the boy? How are these visions connected? If the boy was me, were the other two shadows my parents? Who killed them? Was it Lavenred? Who were the five people in the previous vision? How are they connected? My mind was filled with questions. Was it the future or was it rubbish? I was restless. What was happening? Was I chosen for something? Was it only me chosen among a gazillion lives on Earth? This was not rubbish. It was a vision predicting the future. Were mom and dad going to die? Was this their destiny? This was not the first time when I saw the vision. It was not just a coincidence. It was a pattern. What now? I decided to tell mom and dad.

"Dad," I said, "I want to tell you something."

"What?" dad asked.

"I have had visions twice. It said something weird: that you are going to die, even mom," I said, horrified.

"What? What rubbish!" he said. "Keep quiet! Things like this happen only in movies and books!"

What could I have done? I told the truth already. Now what? Nothing to do but die?

Chapter 9

Losing Somebody- Loneliness

It was only two or three days since I had seen the vision. Nothing happened, but on the evening of the third day, some guards got us out of the jail. It was not just us who were taken out. There were four more families. We were thrown into a van and driven to the parliament house. It was weird. Some of the prisoners were taken to Lavenred.

"Oh! Welcome, Vijay! How is my home? Big and beautiful? Better than your old one?" he said sarcastically. Dad was red with anger and ignored him. "You rat! You are doing so much wrong! Your time will soon come!" dad said, but Lavenred cut him off.

"Shut up! You! Get lost!" he screamed and kicked dad hard on his chest. Dad fell. We were then taken to the basement. The five rooms there were now a kind of special provision. We were thrown together in the third room and locked. Guards stood by the door. After some time, all the rooms were filled. We were shifted from the flats and thrown into the parliament house. My parents were restless. I got scared and saw fear on Dad's face. It was gradually growing. He started sweating.

"Is it about my visions and the prediction I made for you both?" I asked.

"What? Have you totally lost it? No! Nothing like that ever happens! Keep quiet!" he said, exasperated.

"Dad, you can't fool me. I am an equally smart person. I know things like these happen," I cut him off.

He stared at me for a while.

"Anay, come here!" he said, sadly. "We think that things like these happen without warning. Right? Wrong! There are always clues. When President Lincoln was about to die, his photo fell from a table and its glass cracked. He was hit with a bullet on the same place where the glass had cracked. In your case, it's a vision!" he said.

"I can run, but I cannot hide, your mother, too. It is all written. You can't change it!" he said. I was amazed. He told me things I didn't know. Dad was greater than me.

"Mr. Vijay!" a guard said, "Sir Lavenred is calling you!" he said as he opened the jail doors and took him. I managed to get out.

"Mom, I'll be back!" I said and tiptoed behind dad. Dad was taken to Lavenred. Both of them had a long talk. It turned into an argument. I try to remember what had happed then, but it doesn't come to my mind. Lavenred screamed with anger. Both his guards held dad and he took out his sword.

Dad then said, "Nothing will happen by killing me. You need to kill your own death!"

A second later, I heard the sound of my father screaming. I saw blood. Dad died before my eyes. Tears ran down my eyes.

"Dad! No!" I cried and ran to dad from the wall I was hiding behind. I fell beside dad and started crying. "You ...You rat! I swear that whatever happens, you will die in my hands," I said in anger.

"You, will kill me?" Lavenred laughed.

"Yes, you rat! You will die in my hands!" I said in anger. He signaled to his guard. The guard came back with mom.

"Still want to kill me?" he asked. His guard took his sword and placed it at her throat.

"Mom! No!" I screamed. "Lavenred! You cowardly thug, heartless criminal, you do not deserve to live!" I screamed.

He turned angrier and I saw a tearful scene again. This time, I saw my mother die. I cried and fell beside her. She held my hand and died. I was now all alone.

Chapter 10

Taman

It was the worst day. I lost my parents. Lavenred's countdown had begun. Not even God could have saved us now.

"Pick him up and throw him in the dungeon!" Lavenred said. I was thrown into the same basement room. It felt lonelier. I sat in a corner, and felt itchy. I looked around and saw a CD, with my parents' handwriting on it. I kept it with me. I made a light with the batteries, wires and bulbs I had. Being interested in electronics, I always had some of this in my pocket. I had a way of getting out by jumping through doors. I went out, jumping through doors, to get some stuff to make a DVD player. I collected all that I needed: a needle, a wooden base, a motor, wires, USB cables and other things. It took time but I made it. I connected it to my mobile, but never dared to play it. I always thought that a thing like this could always increase my loneliness. What was I to do? Stay, and wait till death came? Or go to Lavenred, kill him for once and for all and then wait for death to come? All alone and helpless, I was planning to kill the world's most powerful man. One night, I sat beside the wall. I heard a knock. This time, it was a boy with a strong voice.

"Hello? Hello? Is there someone out there?" he said.

"Yes. Who are you?" I asked, hesitating.

"I am Taman," he said. He climbed up his wall and entered my cabin. "Who are you and what are you doing here? We must be in our separate cabins. Now go!" I said, afraid.

"Why are you scared? I won't harm you! I am a friend!" he said, consoling me.

"I lost both my parents recently. That swine Lavenred killed them! I have heard about you, Anay. I have also heard that you have sworn to kill him. Is there any truth to this?" he asked.

"Yes. It is true. That cold blooded creature killed my parents, and I swear to kill him!" I said.

"Well, then I guess you can't do this alone, can you?" he asked.

"What do you mean?" I asked, confused, seeing a helpful spark in his eyes.

"I am with you, friend!" he said happily. This couldn't have been happening! I remembered the five shadows in this vision, I guess we were the first two. What was this? Help from God? A destined happening? A plan? It was the precipice of change. The good had dawned upon evil. Soon, there was to be a sunrise.

Chapter 11

Vensolio

I regained some confidence that I lost after my parents' death. Taman was a nice chap. We spent about three to four days together. When the guards came to give us lunch and dinner, he went to his cabin, otherwise, he stayed with me all the time.

"What did you study before all this happened?" He asked me one day.

"Me? Oh, nothing but I was studying science and planned strategies. I am also a chess expert. What about you? What did you study?" I said.

"Me I wish I could say it directly!" he said as he stood up and started walking by the wall.

"What do you mean? You can tell me. I am your best friend, now." I said.

"Okay, fine then. I am a pickpocket." he said, which was a shock.

"What? You are a pickpocket? You steal money?" I said, still smarting under the shock he had given me. "Wait! I am not exactly a pickpocket. I don't steal money from just anyone. It's only select ones who betray me, my friends and family. I don't even use that money. I give it to the one who was cheated. If not, I donate it! Just like Robin hood!" he said, in a single breath. I was still shocked.

"What? This is confusing. I just ..." I had not recovered from a shock like this. I had another shock, in the form of a knock from the other door.

"Hello! Hello! Is somebody there?" I heard a strange voice.

"Yes." I said hesitating, "But who are you?"

"I am Vensolio!" the voice answered.

"VENSOLIO? What? What kind of a name is that?" Taman asked sarcastically. "Wait I'll come and explain," he said. The next minute, I saw a man walk out through the wall!

"Hi! I am Vensolio!" he said in a polished accent. My mouth was wide open, Taman's was, too.

"Did you just walk through the wall?" Taman asked, hardly able to speak.

"Yes!" said Vensolio, "It is one of my many magic tricks. Don't worry, I'll teach you!"

We were still stunned. What was this?

"Why are you still shocked? Treat me as a friend. I'm not at all different! You are Anay, right? I have heard about your parents and your promise. Is it true?" he asked.

"Yes, it is true. I was alone until now, but Taman has joined me. We are ready to kill Lavenred at any cost!" I said, patting Taman's back.

"This is similar to what has happened with me. My parents were killed by Lavenred. Can I join you?" he asked.

"What? Yes of course!" said Taman. I was happy that I had found the third shadow. Only two more to go.

Chapter 12

Alkazar

The same thing happened. We began spending time with Vensolio. He was a jolly person. He was good company. He was about my age, but had the ability to blend in with small children and aged people alike. He turned out to be a great friend. I was with him for five days. He helped me regain the confidence I had lost.

"What did you do before all this happened? What did you study?" Taman asked him.

"I was a student of the Royal Ministry of Magic," he said.

"What? Magic?" he asked.

"Yes!" he said.

"It was a wonderful place. It had flying horses, unicorns, live pictures, talking books and much more. I was educated there," he said, smiling. What he was thinking of was evident from his glasses. I was going to object to him saying that magic did not exist. Now that I had seen a man walking through the wall, I knew I wouldn't have correct arguments.

"Can you show us some magic tricks?" Taman asked, excited.

"Sure, why not? Anything for my best friends!" he said joyfully.

He went to a corner and sat there, moving his lips. Not more than a moment later, he had fire in his hands. He played with it like a child playing with a toy. He closed his hands and blew into it. When he opened his hands, a Phoenix flew out.

"Such a beautiful creature! The Phoenix is the purest form of magic. If it is shot in the heart of a dead person, there is a 50% chance of reviving him, provided his body is fine!" he said, and called the Phoenix back into his hands.

"This is great!" Taman and I said. We heard a huge boom and one of the prison walls exploded. The wall broke into pieces. Through the mist of dust, I saw a shadow. It seemed similar to the one in my vision.

"What's happening? Who is it?" The guards from outside screamed.

"Vensolio! Stop the guards now!" I said, staring at him. He murmured something and froze the

Chapter 26

The Story of Life

We were back on Earth. Now, we had to rule our kingdom. We renounced our kingship, and restored the world to what it used to be before. The Earth then became a changed place. People began resorting to peace rather than war. People changed for the good. They understood that powers were not to be played around with. They were meant to be beyond our reach. That was why further research on the Book of Destiny was forbidden. This occurrence claimed the approval of believers. A new epic was born: The Book of Destiny.

We were rewarded for our achievements. We were awarded by every country for service to humanity. We were famous and respected. But like any other chapter in history, we were forgotten. Then came a time when we remained only in books. Everything legendary about us had died down because we became normal people. We were finally able to avail the luxury of ordinary things. We took decision to disperse. We went away to different places with absolutely no contact with each other. We had no idea where the others were. We left it to the Universe. When the time would come, things would fall in place. We lived with that theory. There was no news of Lavenred. We had no idea where he was or how he was. Though I killed him, I felt that the loop was not over yet. There's more that I need to fulfill before I die. Thinking of it as another dream, I would forget about it. Though I tried to lead my life normally, I would have a lot of questions. Why did dad fight Lavenred? Why did Lavenred behead him? Why was Mom's death necessary? Who was Lavenred? What was the actual identity of my father? What was Vikram talking about when he told me that my visions were a secret for which I was not prepared? Why did the Universe make us immortal? What happened with the Book and Lavenred after we left for Earth? Was the story of The Book of Destiny finished?

These questions forced me to think. With so many loopholes, my story framed up pretty bluntly. With all these questions left unanswered... DO YOU THINK THIS IS WHERE MY STORY ENDS?

"With time, my friend, you will discover answers ..."

We were using our brains. Each time, we came short of only one person. "Ah! God help us with only one more person! We need just one more!" Taman said. "See guys I know that I –" I was just about to complete my sentence when I heard someone sobbing.

"Did everyone hear what I heard?" I asked.

"Someone sobbing?" Alkazar said.

"Yes," Taman and Vensolio said. It was from the next cabin. I knocked the wall, "Is anyone there? I asked.

"Who are you? What do you want from me?" a trembling voice came from the other side.

"It's a girl!" I whispered.

"Excuse me, may I come to you?" I asked gently.

"Will you harm me? Who are you?" she asked again.

"There is no need to worry. We are good people. You never know, we could be of some use to you!" I said to her.

"Okay, fine!" she said.

The next minute, I climbed the wall and jumped into her cabin. She sat in a corner crying.

"What is it? Why are you crying?" I asked her gently as I sat beside her.

"That rogue Lavenred killed my parents!" she said crying.

"What's your name?" I asked her hastily.

"Sanya," she said.

"Sanya do you know that there are three people in the next cabin, including me, making that four, who have faced the same situation? We are getting together to make a plan to kill him. Would you like to join us?" I asked her.

"It would be very helpful."

"I want to kill that rat! I will surely join you!" she said. My satisfaction had risen over the seven skies. We jumped over the wall and entered the room. I had met all five of them. Destiny had brought my team to me. I turned from one to five. Lavenred was now close to his end.

Chapter 14

Another Vision

"This is Sanya!" I introduced her to everyone.

"Sanya, this is Taman, this is Vensolio and this is Alkazar."

"Finally! Someone with a normal name!" Taman said.

"Alkazar is a weird name?" Alkazar asked, wrinkles appearing on his forehead.

"It is the most common name in all of Kingston!"

"What's Kingston?" Taman asked.

"Oh it's a town in Mexico!" Alkazar said.

"Where is Mexico?" Taman asked, confused.

"It's on the Isthmus of Panama," Alkazar answered seriously.

"Now what's Isthmus of Panama?" Taman asked, frustrated.

"It is the land that joins North and South America!" Alkazar answered, doubly frustrated. Sanya heard the argument and giggled.

"You guys are funny!" she said.

"Oh these guys? This keeps happening!" I said. She became happier. Sanya blended in with us. She was shy, but enjoyed good company. She was an Expert of the Eagle in Kung-fu. I was a Champion in Tiger. Taman was as sharp as a Hawk. Vensolio was a Grasshopper and Alkazar was a Gorilla.

She was perfectly balanced between jolliness and seriousness. She wrote poetry. We had many things in common. She also was a kind of a doctor, and knew pressure points on which if one were to press, they could give life to a person whose heart has stopped, within ten to fifteen minutes of its stoppage. She gained all the confidence she had lost. One evening, Vensolio had given us coffee, and we sat down to talk, laughing and giggling. I suddenly felt a chill pass through my spine. The laughter seemed to diminish. My vision started to blow, and numbness took over my body. It was a vision, again. Everything blackened before my eyes, and a brown screen unfolded. I saw five shadows displayed, and I vaguely guessed that it was Taman, Vensolio, Alkazar, Sanya and me. We stood, and crowns appeared on our heads. We disappeared gradually, and then, I saw Lavenred. He was picked up by two shadows – probably guards – who threw him out of his castle. The five of us had entered the castle. Slowly, the screen cleared out. Then, I saw The Book of Destiny. It was open, and something was written on its pages. It was unclear and I could not read. Suddenly, there was a spark of eight. The Book started to replicate itself. In the end, there were two like books that read "The Book of Destiny". Gradually, the screen started blackening. It went dark.

What was the meaning of these crowns? What did they symbolise? What was the castle? Why was Lavenred on the streets? Who threw him there? What was he doing there? Where were his guards? What was written in the book? Who wrote it? Why did it replicate itself? What did it mean? Was it a clue to make a plan to get the book? Many questions came to mind, and were all unanswered. I woke up from the dream suddenly. I was still too restless to understand what was happening. I shivered and my mind went numb. What was the vision for?

"I … I … I… ju … Just … just s … saw…" I shivered and hesitated.

"No! Wait. This pressure could burst a nerve in your head. Rest now and explain it later," Sanya said, feeling my forehead. My temperature seemed high. I went to my cabin. Vensolio made a hole in the wall so I could go through. When I went, he closed it behind me. I was sick because of the vision.

"What did … w … what … di … did those books mean?" I asked myself. Before I could think, I fell asleep.

Chapter 15

The Plan

I slept for a long time that night. I didn't know what had happened that night. The next day, when I woke up, my head felt heavy. I woke up late, at around nine or ten in the morning. Everyone had breakfast in my cabin. Sanya was dull.

"What happened to you?" I asked her.

"Nothing, yet!" She replied normally. "Okay come on. She was up all night keeping a check on you. She felt that you might end up having a brain hemorrhage!" Taman said. "Did you, really?" I asked Sanya. "Yes. What were you trying to tell us last night?" she asked.

"Oh … Yesterday? No … I … ah … saw … saw the … Ah leave it! Tell me the plan you have all made," I said.

"Oh, the plan! We haven't made one yet," Vensolio said.

"What were you doing all the time?" I asked.

"Oh, yesterday? Nothing. Just having fun! We had dinner and slept. I thought it would be better if all of us, including you, will sit together to discuss the plan," Alkazar said.

"Oh my gosh! Do you even realize you have wasted a whole night?" I said, surprised, trying to settle what looked like a conflict. "You could have completed it then!"

"We are just starting," Vensolio said. We ate our breakfast and sat together to discuss the plan.

"So these are who we have: a scientist, a chemistry expert, a pickpocket, a magician, and a Kung-fu artist," Vensolio said.

"What can be done with these five?" Taman asked.

"Tomorrow morning, we will enter our own cabins. When the guards come, Alkazar will make a lot of noise. The guards will go to his cabin. Taman will then go to the guards and steal keys from them. If they realize that Taman is behind them, Vensolio will freeze them and Sanya will cut them in the neck. Vensolio will free us," I said.

"What about the book? I have heard that he keeps the book in a secret room?" Taman said.

"He keeps it in a room that can only be opened by Lavenred himself. The lane where the room is, is completely secured by guards. When we get out, it will be tea time for Lavenred. We will hypnotize the guard and send him with tea to Lavenred!" I said, using my experience with him.

"But the door can only be opened by his voice!" Sanya said, confused.

"When Lavenred will tell the guard to pour sugar, we will record his voice."

"How do you know he'll ask him to pour sugar?" Vensolio asked.

"Vensolio, my friend! he has been coming home for about eight years. I know how he drinks his tea!" I replied sharply.

"Vensolio will listen to his voice and use it to unlock the door. He will make all the guards unconscious so that we can go inside. Then, Alkazar will use his chemicals to melt the bulletproof glass. After we enter the room, I'll get the book and we will run. If it does not happen the way we plan it, and all the guards wake up, Sanya and I will take care of them. By that time, you three should take the book and run," I said.

"Everything has been taken care of. It's a great plan. We have a backup here. I think we should go with it!" Vensolio said. Everyone agreed. The plan making was not as difficult as I thought. But all is well that ends well. Everyone was waiting for was the next morning. Though the plan was theoretically perfect, we were sound about the execution. Nobody knew what the future was going to hold for us. All we could do was to wait.

Chapter 16

The Book Stolen

The moment we were waiting for had finally come. We woke up early and had our breakfast. The guards had come. We went to our cabins. Everything happened per schedule. Alkazar started his work.

"Hey, you two! Ugly, fat creatures! Come here! Your bodies stink!" he yelled.

With utmost cat–like smoothness, Taman climbed the prison grills. Alkazar was doing well, distracting the guards. They were too distracted to notice what Taman was doing. Making no sound at all, Taman jumped out of prison. The keys were hung on the belt of the second guard. Taman used his long and flexible fingers to get the keys. He succeeded.

"Good Job!" I whispered. Taman, overconfident after his success, bowed formally. What he didn't realize was that the keys were stuck in the bars and clanged noisily. His smile changed to a frown – he knew what was going to happen next.

“Hey you! Give back the keys!” one of the guards said.

“Vensolio! Now!” Taman screamed. Vensolio suspended the guards in their position. Meanwhile, Taman freed Sanya. When Vensolio freed the guards, Sanya punched them hard on their faces. They were down in an instant.

“That went well!” Vensolio said, as Taman freed all of them. The second phase of the plan began. Vensolio picked up a guard and wiped the blood off his nose. He said something into his ears with his eyes closed. The guard got up. He was in our control. It was exactly 10:00 AM, and thirty minutes had gone. We had six minutes to go. The guard picked up the tea and was on his way.

This was the tough part. We had to control the guard in such a way that it seemed normal. It was challenging because it was not a normal pathway. It was well watched by guards. If even one guard noticed something fishy, we were as good as gone. I guess such a situation did not come. Being an expert in his art, Vensolio did his job well. We saw what was happening. Soon, we reached Lavenred’s room. The guard walked in with tea. We waited for Lavenred to speak up. “Sugar, please!” Lavenred said in his usual tone. Our faces lit up with smiles. “I told you!” I whispered into Vensolio’s ear “Yes, but how much?" He asked. "Two Spoons!" the guard put two spoons of sugar in the tea. He left the room. We walked the guard back to us. "Hey Alkazar! We need a solution that can temporarily burn the eyes of the guards. Like tear gas," I said. "You got it boss!" He said and got busy with his chemicals. Vensolio made us some masks. Alkazar was ready with the gas. We ran to the room where the book of Destiny was placed. Alkazar set the bomb ablaze. The guards screeched, rubbing their eyes. Sanya and I managed to finish them.

By the time we were done, Vensolio concentrated on the next part: opening the gates. "You're up, boy! Don't let us down!" I said. Vensolio opened his eyes, signaling that he was ready. He bent forward and said, "Open the gates!" I stared at him with my jaw open. The voice was an exact copy of Lavenred's, just as heavy and dull. The gates opened, and we had almost reached our goal. Between the book and us, there was a bullet proof glass. It was up to Alkazar once again. "Melt it!" I said. He held it. But he seemed nervous, as if something was disturbing him. He looked through me, as though I was transparent. His face showed the effort he was trying to make to win the war between two unknown elements inside his heart. He broke away from his thoughts and began doing what he was supposed to do.

He signed and started working with the chemicals. It looked like he was concentrating on what he was doing fully, but it was not so. He used only half his brains, while the rest remained numb. I couldn't tell what he was thinking, but with a faint outline it seemed like guilt. I don't know what happened there: call it bad luck, or ill fate or pre-written destiny, but Alkazar was ready with the wrong solution. He poured it on the glass. Instead of melting, it burst. The alarms went off. In no time, the place was flooded with guards. "What have you done?" Vensolio exclaimed. Alkazar could not speak. He looked through Vensolio. We had nothing else to do aside of fighting the guards. Everyone was in position, except Alkazar, who was shaken. We fought the guards. I realized that just fighting them would not help. I picked up a sharp piece of glass and cut my finger. I opened the book and wrote on it: "a pen". I read it aloud. A pen appeared. By this time, Lavenred was already in the room. He was alone, since all his guards were either dead or unconscious and we were five in number. "I should have known! You will all end up like your parents, now!" He exclaimed and came to fight. Sanya, Vensolio and Taman fought him back. Alkazar was too lost to do anything. I was busy with the book.

"Anay, Taman, Vensolio, Alkazar and Sanya take over Lavenred's empire and he comes down to the streets," I wrote on the book. Lavenred was busy fighting the trio. Alkazar was in his own world. Our cards were much stronger than Lavenred's. I stood up and read what I had written out loud. "No!" Lavenred said as he pushed back the three and came to me. I threw the book at Sanya and got ready to fight Lavenred. He jumped on to me and I fought back with equal vigor. I expressed my anger. It was a tough fight. Nevertheless, I managed to knock him down. Meanwhile, everything changed. The power was back with us. Lavenred had lost. Out of nowhere, two guards came, but they were ours. "Take him, and throw him outside!" I said to them. They did as told. "I will be back!" he exclaimed. Evil had lost, and good triumphed

Chapter 17

The Real Meaning – Replicated Book

"That went well!" Vensolio said as he came towards me. I swallowed my anger and smiled. Sanya was happy. So was Taman. But Alkazar was still out of his senses. "We made it happen!" I said happily.

"Absolutely, King Anay!" Taman said, smiling.

"King? Wow! I guess that is what success sounds like," I said.

Alkazar was still uninvolved. He sat in a corner, blank. I decided not to talk to him immediately, and not to let anyone else either.

"He needs time. He will be alright in a few hours. Just minor shock!" I told them. "Okay. By the way, we won't have to stay in these cells anymore! Let's look at our new rooms, shall we?" Vensolio said. Taman and Sanya followed him. I stood starting right at Alkazar. My warmth was gone. I looked at him with a frown on my face.

"Do you plan on staying here?" Sanya asked.

"I'll come!" I said, breaking away from my thoughts. I walked ahead And Alkazar still there. He continued to stare into space. I thought something was wrong. Why was he still sad? We had won, but why so much sadness? I wondered why I should bother. Let's rejoice! We had won!

"You guys go, I'll be with you soon," I said. I went to my room and picked up the CD and went to them. Lavenred was on the streets. All five of us ruled. Everything that was happening was according to the vision. There was only one mystery – what was the signal given by both the books? It was still a mystery.

It had now been two or three weeks to our victory. We would now get lavish dinners, breakfasts and lunches like never before. With all comforts on one side, we were now politically that most powerful people on Earth! We ruled it. All prisoners were free. All buildings were checked and used as houses again. The roads began to be crowded again. Gardens echoed with laugher of children. All that had been snatched had been duly restored and returned. Things grew normal. With Lavenred on the streets, there was nobody to stop us. We had no one to fear. We had meetings with the public each evening and talked about the difficulties they faced.

We listened to them, and acted on them. People were happy, and so were we. Things were not as smooth with Alkazar. He was quiet all the time, and did not indulge in conversation. He did not laugh as he usually did. One day, when dinner was ready, I said to Sanya, "Dinner is ready. Let's go!" "Yes. I will get there. Let the meeting finish!" she said. It was a tough day. Everyone finally came to the dinner table. Gradually, food was served. "What delicacies! This is the best food I have ever tested!" Taman exclaimed. Everyone agreed him. Something was disturbing Alkazar. He was fidgeting with his spoon. Why would a man who was the jolliest, sit in such a pensive mood?

"Can I have a word with you, Alkazar, if you don't mind?" I asked. "Yes sure! But why?" he asked.

"Come with me!" I said, pushing my chair back. I went with Alkazar to a secret place. He came behind me. I had figured out what the problem was. Alkazar was still serious.

"Hello! Mr. Fake!" I said to him.

"Mr. Fake?" he asked, hesitating.

"Yes. You know, right?" I asked him.

"What?" he asked, afraid. "The book is replicated!" I said angrily,

"You also know that the book of Destiny is replicated. What did you think?"

"Yes, I knew!" he said hesitating again.

"Kingston, out of all the places?" I asked Alkazar. He tried his best to pretend that he didn't know what I was talking about. But he couldn't keep it from me. "I see your approach now. Make it look realistic. Make it detailed yet simple, and people will believe it. Am I right?" I asked, my temper rising.

"I don't know what you are talking about!" he said, hesitating.

"Oh you know well what I am talking about. You disguise yourself under a nearly laughable name and have an equally pathetic story which you think will be your justification, and yet you think you could hide it from me? You fool!" I said.

"No, you are not Mexican. You are an Indian. You are no Alkazar! You are Vikram. You are not even one of us. You are a man sent by Lavenred. I won't be surprised to know that all that happened was a part of his plan!"

"I did not tell anyone about our plan, believe me. How do you know all this?" He asked. I looked at him, and his head was lowered because of his guilt.

"Do you think you are the only one in disguise?" He looked up, confused.

"What do you mean? I am not the only one?" He asked. I looked at him for a while.

"I am not a scientist. I am a telepath. I can read and control minds," I said. His jaw dropped out of shock. He recovered, and opened his mouth to say something. I looked at him. He stared at me for a moment.

"Am I busted? Will you throw me out, or you want me to do that myself?" he said with a voice laden with sorrow and regret.

"I am a traitor as equal as you are. Technically, I didn't have moral authority to do that," I said.

"I will go then!" he nodded and turned to leave.

"Wait!" I said. "You have done something wrong, agreed. But I saw the guilt in you. I saw it the day we defeated Lavenred. I have been seeing it since. You have that urge to change for good. That neutralizes this situation. As a punishment, you have to bear with us a little longer," I said, smiling. He smiled back with a tear in his eye.

"Thank you, brother!" he said, as he hugged me. We had Alkazar back, finally. "What do we have to tell them? What about our identities?" Alkazar asked.

"We will tell them, but not now. We will wait for the right time. Till then, continue with this face," I said.

"So what do we do now?" Vikram asked. "I guess we will have our dinner!" I said, laughing.

"Yeah! Sure!" he said joyfully.

"Hey guys! See! Alkazar's back in character!" Sanya exclaimed. We had dinner and went to sleep.

Chapter 18

The Real Meaning - The CD

Everyone went to their rooms to sleep. It was a dark night with a deadly silence. I tried to sleep, but something pinched my mind. I wasn't able to point out what it was. I felt uncomfortable, so I switched on the lights and sat up. I saw a CD on my table. I recollected all that I knew about the CD. Maybe it was the only thing that disturbed me. I went to play it. But something stopped me. Was it fear? Or was it guilt? I wanted to reveal the secrets in the CD, but my conscience stopped me. I lost the protracted battle with my fear. My hands hadn't gathered the power to pick up that thing. Thinking that it was so late at night, I ignored it and tried to sleep. But sleep itself was miles away from my eyes. The fear was not allowing me to sleep. I even tried to do the most boring thing, but sleep was still not convinced. It was one of my sleepless nights. I didn't even know what was in the CD, but still I wasn't able to control my fear. Was it only because that mom and dad had made it that stopped me? The night passed with these thoughts running in my mind. My alarm cut into my thoughts, and it was time for me to wake up. Well, not really wake up, because I hadn't slept. Till breakfast, everything was normal.

"Why are you so tense?" Sanya asked me at the breakfast table. "No, nothing like that," I said, hesitating and fidgeting with my fork. It was a good breakfast. But I felt something was missing something. Not in the food, but in my life. I was, maybe, missing my parents. I still was not prepared to watch what was on that CD. I feared it might increase my loneliness, though I was in good company. The ten grams heavy CD was proving to be very heavy for my hands. I had two options: to listen to the CD or not. I was confused. I closed my eyes and tried to see my parents, and all the happy moments we spent together gave me strength and confidence. I went to my room and picked up the CD and put it in the player. I picked up the remote, and was just about to press play. I stopped for a moment and wondered if I was doing right. I smiled to myself and played it. There was a long silence for some time. Each second seemed to be long drawn.

"Son," it began with Dad's voice. "If you have this with you, you are on the right path." Dad's voice brought tears to my eyes.

"I know what you are going through. But you should not fall. Nothing big has happened by my death. If you have a clean heart, I continue living there. Whenever you feel insecure, think of your parents and convert yourself. My death is very close. I don't know if this message will be useful to you, but I still say, never be greedy. Greed will lead you to death, especially when you are against Lavenred. You need to focus. I am proud of you, my son. Goodbye!" It ended and went blank. I was in tears, missing them so much. I wished I could rewind every moment I spent with them. I was lost in thought. But now, I had my father in a CD. It didn't decrease my loneliness, but it helped me throw out all the pain in my heart. I felt light, and realized how much my parents loved me. It was afternoon by the time I was done. I felt light and happy. I had no plans for the rest of the day. I sat in the car and went out on the streets. I saw children playing in the park. It reminded me of my childhood. On the way, I saw a child being scolded by his father, and remembered how my father used to scold me. He would then give me a big hug. The child was so lucky to have a father and so lucky to be called son.

When I got back, it was late evening. I went out in the garden and lay down in the open. I watched the stars, hoping that the cool breeze would blow, reminding me of some of my best moments with my parents. I was satisfied. My parents were happy and satisfied somewhere. It was a strange feeling of happiness. I can't explain it in words. I slept, and finally, it was a satisfied sleep.

Chapter 19

Rise of the Evil Empire

I slept well, and woke up late that morning to what appeared to be a great day. Or did I say that too early? I had never experienced sleeping under gazillion stars in the night sky. The two most shiny stars, my parents, tried to tell me thousands of things. Who knew that a CD can prove to be so motivating!

I really enjoyed the morning too. "Where were you all night?" asked Sanya when she saw me. "I was spending the night with my parents," I replied happily. Everyone watched, confused. I walked to my room. It was pretty late. I lay down on my bed. It was around noon. I was still on my bed. I couldn't help smiling, thinking of what my mother would say for my laziness. "Get up you lazy thing! Go and freshen up!" My smile grew broader as I thought of it. I got up and went to the washroom. It was now late afternoon and I was reading a very interesting book. It was about a boy who had gone to another dimension, because of a man he had killed long world! I leave this to you to take up. I am breaking the deal, do you get it?" Sharma shouted and went away. Dad didn't seem to mind. He picked up the book. It was titled "The Book of Destiny". He didn't care about Sharma's anger that much. It was a piece of cake for him to convince him to renegotiate the deal. What he was worried about was that all that had happened was not normal. He felt that at forty-nine, he was not at an age for adventure. I knew it was late, and I knew that he was overworked. But, I was sure that something else was disturbing him. When he came home, he went straight to sleep without a word with anyone. Everyone thought he was asleep, but he was pretending. At around midnight, he got up and placed the book in the library. It was a smart move. He checked if anyone was around. When the coast was clear, he went to his room. This was again a big mistake which could have been avoided. It had now begun. The Book of Destiny had been discovered.

Chapter 5

The Secret Revealed

This was in 2023, when I was twenty-three. It had then been three years since the book was discovered. Since the library was huge, it could have only been a coincidence by which the book was discovered. Dad had completely forgotten about it. I had no idea either. The book had the power to control the world and was licking dust, while a useless textbook was being used every day. It was a sunny day in the middle of summer: the day I wished had never come. I had nothing to do those days. I loved to read. That day, I was bored and felt like reading something. I walked lazily past the corridor into the library. I looked for a book to read, but for a while, didn't find anything I hadn't already read. Finally, I found The Book of Destiny. I picked it up and found a layer of dust on it. I cleared it with my hand. The cover read "The Book of Destiny" This was not amongst the books I had read. I picked up the book and went back to my room. I spent some time just observing the book. It

"But I want them now!" I cut him off in immense anger. He was still calm. He had the body of a warrior and the brain of a sage. I was surprised by his control over himself. "Fine. Tell me where your brain is situated."

"My head."

"Your head. Absolutely right. You have your body with you, but you cannot feel it. I am inside your mind. This conversation is happening inside your head. It is a dream. A dream that I have given you … By controlling your mind. Maybe the book you were reading in the noon was not impractical."

"You … you control my …. You control my mind?" I asked, surprised.

"Yes."

"But how?"

"The time will come, my boy, the time will come for you to know."

"Reading minds Is a forbidden art! Only a law breaker can do it. The one I know who does that is…" my eyes grew wide in terror, "… the one I know who does that is Lavenred!" I looked for words. My anger had gotten the better of me.

"You filthy animal! I am disgusted to talk to you." Something inside me told me that this wasn't

Lavenred. But I was won over by anger, and couldn't notice it. "Not all who do this are law breakers!"

His voice trembled, as though he was crying, "Especially not me, my son…"

The anger vanished in a second. My eyes were filled with tears. I knew what I had to say, but my throat was choked. I was trembling

"Dad?" I said, with a soft whimper that my choked throat allowed me to use.

"Yes, my son. I am your father." Slowly, my dad emerged before me.

"Son!" he gave me a tight hug. Both of us were choked in emotion.

"I missed you so much! Why didn't you do this earlier?" I asked.

"Everything has a time," he said, his voice calm again.

"Now it is time to tell you …"

"What?"

Dad was hesitating a lot.

"It's time you reveal yours and Alkazar's identity!" he said.

"The time has come. If you say it later, it may be too late!" said dad.

"Why can't you come with me? It will be great. Together, we can defeat anyone easily! Even Lavenred!" I said. Dad smiled with desire in his eyes.

"I would love to, my son. But I am not alive. I can't go into the real world. I will come to meet you frequently," he said, controlling his tears. We watched Dad walk away. I was too busy controlling my tears to stop him. Gradually, it all disappeared. I felt a sudden jerk in my head. A numbness set in and began growing. I saw the same old brown screen. It was another vision. A shadow appeared. Behind it was an army, a huge one. The shadow headed towards a big building, perhaps a castle. It looked familiar. Out of it, appeared five shadows. They seemed to be known, too. An army appeared from behind them too. Both armies faced each other now, like the set up for a war. There seemed to be a conversation between those shadows. One among the five took out something and started writing. There was a bright flash. Everything became visible after some time. It was the two armies again. But the background was different. Both armies began fighting. My vision stared to blur. The screen was black now. My sight darkened completely. I felt a smack on my head, and gradually opened my eyes. My sight, though blurred, was back now. I saw my friends. I was finally awake.

"Hey … what …" I was down again.

Chapter 21

Identities Revealed

"Hey Anay! Wake up!" Sanya said. I opened my eyes slowly. Everyone was sitting in my room.

"Why are you all so worried? It's like you have all held your breath for a long time!" I said in a dry voice, as I picked up a glass of water. "Good to see you awake! It's like we were carrying a mountain on our shoulders. Now it has gone!" said Vensolio, happily.

"Why are you acting in weird? What is there to be surprised about? A boy went to sleep and woke up!" I asked, with a chuckle.

"Not exactly NORMAL sleep."

"What?"

"I mean that you have been asleep for about three days!" Vensolio said.

"What? Three days! Are you serious?"

"Yes, that's why we all were tense!" Said Sanya, "How are you now?"

"Me? Better than ever!" I said with a smile.

"You've been asleep for three days. I bet it was something that you saw, something serious. Tell us what it was," said Taman.

"I expected this from you, Taman!" I said with a smile. "What I saw was not something you will believe!" This time I was serious.

"Do you know who I saw?" I asked. Everyone was silent.

"It was my father. He says there are many secrets we still do not know. Anything can happen," I said.

"And he told me to reveal a secret," I hesitated, as I stared into Alkazar's eyes. He understood what I wanted to say. He was as hesitant as me now.

"It is that Alkazar and I are…"

"Are what?" asked Taman. "We …. We are not who you think we are!"

"What do you mean?" Sanya asked.

"We will reveal our identities," I said, gathering courage.

"Your real identities? What do you mean?" Vensolio said, now getting serious.

"I am no Scientist. I am ... a ..." I was cut off.

"Oh! Stop hesitating! Just say it!" Taman said, unable to control his exasperation. I gathered my wits and courage.

"I am not a scientist. I'm a telepath."

Jaws dropped in surprise. There was complete silence in the room. Everyone wanted to speak, but their throats were choked. They couldn't find words to speak. Everyone was shocked. They sank under fear and excitement. You become friends with a person, spend a lot of time with him and suddenly discover that he has a completely different identity – this can be shocking for anyone!

"You are a telepath? How can this be possible?" Sanya said, breaking the silence.

"Yes!"

"But .... How...."

"Why? Isn't telepathy science?"

"Yes it is but ...."

"What?"

"How can you betray us?" asked Taman.

"This is no betrayal!" said Alkazar, with tears in his eyes. "The real traitor is me!"

"What?" asked Vensolio, unprepared for another surprise.

"No! You are not! You ..."

"Stop! Stop hiding the truth, Anay! Don't you remember what your father said?" Alkazar asked.

"What are you talking about, Alkazar?" Taman asked.

"I am not Alkazar."

"What do you mean?"

"My real name is Vikram," he said. "I not from Kingston. I am not from Mexico. I am Indian." "How come you" Sanya asked, but choked midway with emotion. "I am from Lavenred's army!" he said.

"You are an enemy!" Vensolio said, seemingly in a state of deep shock. "I know! I hate myself! I betrayed you! I betrayed my best friends! I am sick of myself!" Vikram said, bursting into tears. "Vikram. It's okay. It's just ..." Taman said, "NO! IT IS NOT! I AM LEAVING! I DON'T EVEN WANT TO LIVE! I WILL PUNISH MYSELF! I AM GOING AWAY TO LIVE WITHOUT ALL OF YOU!" Vikram said, dashing out of the room. Everyone was in tears. Happiness had turned in to hatred.

Chapter 22

The Feeling of Loneliness Returns

Sadness had taken over. What could have been done? Our identities were like huge guns that fired back on us. Nobody had seen Alkazar for a long time. It was late at night, and sleep was far away. Every face there wore an expression of gloom. Nobody had recovered from the shock. Everything was going great before this, was it still written somewhere? May be on the torn pages of the book? Or perhaps, a book even greater than the book of destiny did exist! Vikram locked himself in his room. Everyone tried to knock or break in, but nobody could. Vikram was smart, he had a strong mind. I tried to see what he was thinking, but was always obstructed. I couldn't understand why. I was sure that Vikram wasn't planning on running away, because he knew that he could be brought back in the blink of an eye with the book. What else could he have done? Maybe .... Maybe, resort to death? With this thought, my eyes widened and my heart started thumping loudly. I panicked. I used my might and power to break the door. Vikram was sitting on the chair near his bed, and seemed to be terribly sad. His eyes still had tears. Seeing him alive, I was satisfied. But I felt sad for him, seeing him in such a bad condition. He didn't even sense our presence. We decided not to disturb him, and decided to walk away. While walking away, for a moment, I saw a screen. Something started moving on it. It seemed to a shadow of a man, and appeared to be walking out of a huge building – perhaps a castle. Four people stood behind, looking at the walking one. One of the shadows ran forward, as if it was trying to stop him. Suddenly, there was a huge eruption. The one who walked away vanished. The one who was behind him seemed hurt. The other three were motionless. The screen then went blank, and soon it was black. Was this another vision? Who was that shadow? Where had it gone? What had happened? What was that huge eruption? Was it related to any happening in the future? Who was the shadow running behind? Who caused this eruption?

Was it related to Vikram? The shocking thought woke me up. It was morning, and I realized that I had slept. I woke everyone, one by one. We went to Vikram's room. I was still horrified. I kicked open the door and was flabbergasted by what I saw. The room was empty! There was a note on Vikram's bed. It read "Goodbye. If possible, please forgive me. – Vikram." My eyes filled with tears. We dashed out of his room and entered the main passage. I saw Vikram walking away. We ran after him. Soon, we were out of the Castle. Vikram was still in sight. "Vikram! Stop!" I shouted, but he couldn't hear me. I ran to stop him, though I knew the consequences.

I saw something fall from the sky as I ran. It was blackish-red and huge. My eyes opened wide. It was a bomb! It was near Vikram. "Vikram! Look out!" I screamed. But it was already too late. The bomb had fallen, and the huge explosion tossed me away to the side. I was fine, but my eyes were wet. My heart felt like it would come out of my throat. "Vikram!" I screamed, but heard nothing in response. There was nothing in sight. I tried to run, but noticed that my left leg was bleeding. Somehow, I used my feet, and staggered through the dust, with an aimless hope to find Vikram alive. But there was no sign of him! We had lost Vikram. It reminded me of the day we lost our parents. I had now lost a brother. Loneliness had arrived again.

Chapter 23

The Thought of Vengeance

Everyone was sitting in the room. It was completely silent. Everyone's eyes were red with anger. Who knew that such a thing was going to happen? What could have been done?

"Revenge!" Taman said. There was rage in his voice. Sanya was disturbed, and was panicking. "N …. No!" she said, crankily. "It is not done. I am as worried, angry and vengeful like you all!" "But why? Do we sit here and do nothing?" asked Vensolio, sounding angrier. "No! This is not going the right way! Please!" Sanya said. I cut in, "Find that filthy rat!" Sanya was a bit relieved. "Find him and tear off every part of him! He will be avenged. Vikram will be brought to justice!" I said. My mind had blown into a gazillion pieces thanks to my anger, "That shameless pig has blown our friend up! We couldn't even see him off! He will be avenged. He will pay for what that rat has done. He shall be killed," I said, as a tear rolled down my cheek.

Sanya was now speechless. She was surprised at my reaction. I was surprised too. But, anyone who looked into my eyes could see what I was saying. This was above all anger, above all rage. I was still in control. Anyone else might have died from a high blood pressure. But now, there was nothing left to do. The last resort was war.

"Equip yourselves with all your weapons. Signal our forces to prepare themselves. We're off to Lavenred's Empire!" I said, making a harsh but necessary decision. We went to the book. "Where is Lavenred? Show us a map where Lavenred is!" I wrote in it and read aloud. The ink began disappearing. Suddenly, in front of me, there appeared a map showing us where Lavenred was. "Now pack up your things and get ready! We're off to Lavenred," I said. I was relieved that in a matter of some time, I could end what had begun two decades ago. I could find some boring and normal time then. "We're on!" Taman said, with a crooked smile. "Let's go!" I said. We left the castle and went where Lavenred was.

Chapter 24

Meet with the Mastermind

I knew Lavenred very well. He was cunning. His broad smile still sent shudders through me. I thought it was all going according to his plan. I felt that someone was keeping an eye on us and that we were being watched. But how did he know we were on the way to reach him? It was dark at night. The only light was the full moon and the dim stars twinkling beside it. I felt uneasy and uncomfortable, and had a constant feeling that someone was watching our movements. I felt holes in my back from some watchful eye somewhere. I looked around, but saw nothing in sight, save for plants and trees that stretched as far as my eyes could see.

"We will reach Lavenred's Castle by tomorrow, if we go in this direction," Sanya said, looking into a small machine and pointing her arms towards the North. "Then let's not be foolish! Let's rest right now," I said.

"But why?" Taman asked. "If we keep walking, we will be half-dreaming with aching limbs when we see Lavenred tomorrow!" Vensolio said, reading my mind. We sat around a campfire that we set up. We had some hot dogs to eat.

"Vikram would have loved these hot-dogs," Sanya said. Her eyes were blank. "Yeah, with him gone, I do not feel life in myself," Vensolio said in a trembling voice.

"Yes. Despite being foolish, he was the life within us!" Taman said, as a tear rolled down his cheeks. I was speechless. I felt the same, and I could understand how they felt. We had our snack and went on our journey. We walked the whole night and reached his castle. It was a huge grey coloured fortress. Huge! Lavish! Luxurious! The filthy rat had no right to stay in such a home, made by killing tons of innocent people!

"Here lives that filthy rat!" I said, as my face turned crimson.

"What do we do now? How do we get in?" someone asked. I examined the trees around, and found the one I was looking for. "Keep a gun on that tree, and aim at a guard," I said. Vensolio went there, and placed the gun.

"Now what?" Taman asked. "Now we go to the opposite point," I said. We walked to the opposite side and it was not far.

"What do you plan to do, Anay?" Sanya asked. I will shoot at the trigger of the gun placed atop the tree. It will hit a guard. The remaining guards will come and search for the criminal on the opposite side. No one will search here and we will enter the fortress," I said.

"Superb!" Vensolio said. "Ready?" I asked.

"Shoot!" Taman said. In no time, I shot the bullet, and it hit the trigger of the other gun. The other gun's bullet went straight into a guard's back. There was panic. Everyone crowded near the dead one, and started searching for the shooter. Meanwhile, we went inside the castle. It was beautiful. The coward was living in luxury. We entered a huge room, plated with black colored tiles. On a raised platform was a tall black chair with two guards standing beside it. "Welcome!" said a deep and heavy voice from behind the chair. "Long time since we have met, right?" The voice said again. It was LAVENRED! The moment I recognized his voice, I went crimson with rage. I felt like killing him right there, but his guards held us immediately, and seized our weapons.

"Why did you do that?" I asked, crimson in rage.

"What?"

"YOU KNOW!" I shouted. "Why did you kill Vikram! Didn't you feel disgusted? After killing our parents, you killed an innocent guy!" I screamed. "I challenge you to a war," I said, calming down. Everyone stared at me their jaws open. "Do you or do you not accept my challenge you filthy coward?" I shouted.

"Yes I do!" he said, "It will happen on the day you decide."

"It will happen on the same date of the next month."

"Fine. Go and prepare for your death," he said. We were sent out of the castle. A huge war was coming.

Chapter 25

The Long Awaited War

We were back in our castle. Our forces were trained. We had about 10 million warriors: about 5 million on foot, 2 million on Horses and 3 million archers and shooters. The date of the war drew close and we grew nervous. Would everything happen the right way? What if we lost? What if Lavenred acquired the world again? The day finally arrived. We were on the battle field. There was nothing in sight for some time, until suddenly, when there was some activity far away. When things got closer, it was clearly visible. A huge army had come prepared. They were Lavenred's fighters. They settled, ready for battle. They had a strong army. Surprisingly, they had 5 million warriors on foot, 2 million horses, and about the same number of archers and shooters. They also had 10 million soldiers. If such a war took place on earth, imagine what would have happened! Gazillions of innocent people would have died. The lands would have turned red with the blood of people. In short, it would have been the end of the human race. I had to, at any cost, prevent it from happening.

"Before the war starts, we have certain demands," I shouted in the quiet battlefield. "You may proceed," Lavenred shouted in his deep voice.

"If such a strong battle has to be waged, it cannot take place on earth because millions of innocent lives are at stake. We want this battle to be done away from the universe."

"Write it in the book and it will come true," Lavenred said. I opened the book and started writing: "Take us away from the universe where we shall fight and none living on this earth shall be harmed" and then read it aloud. Everything began to vanish. Letter by letter, word by word, sentence by sentence and then gone. Suddenly, the scene began to fade. Gradually, it all had gone black. I was gob smacked. There was only the opponent army and my army in sight. "This is the place you were looking for," Lavenred said. "Now begin the war."

There was a moment of silence. I examined the war scene again. "What are we waiting for?" I asked.

"Take your formations! Now!" Vensolio exclaimed. We had a four troupe strong concave front. Each troupe was lead by one of us. Lavenred, the coward, sat on a high stone and ordered his army to attack. The commander was named Smarach Maroonie. He was a well built and cunning man. It was not easy for our army to penetrate and maneuver through Lavenred's troupe formations that were designed by Maroonie himself. Both armies rushed at each other. Maroonie's troupes attacked us. We chose to stay in the defense. They used nuclear weapons, some which were horrifying. Vensolio was successful in creating a shield around us. Maroonie's troupes failed with their attack. For the first eleven hours of battle, nothing harmed us. Maroonie, who was now at the back end of the army, was not happy about what was happening. He left the arena and went to Lavenred. "Sir, our attacks are not working!" he said. "I am able to see that," Lavenred said in his as usual tone. "What do you plan to do now? We cannot afford to lose," He repeated. "Sir I want half the army to travel with me. I am heading to the back-end of their army. We will attack from both ends and that way they will be sandwiched," Maroonie said. "Okay! Take the number of men you want to," Lavenred said. "I have a problem. They should not see us going. We need to be transported without being seen," Maroonie said. "That is why I have The Book of Destiny," Lavenred said, "Now go prepare your troupes."

Meanwhile, on the battle field, there was no danger for us. We were guarded well by Vensolio's shield. Maroonie returned to the battlefield. There was something unusual – many soldiers, around half his army, stopped attacking. They made a semi circular formation. In the centre, was Maroonie. He was smiling. "What the hell does he think he is doing?" Sanya asked. "This is confusing. Maybe a retreat?" Taman said. "No. This is something else. Let me see!" I said, and looked at Maroonie, right into his eyes. I placed my fingers on my temple and closed my eyes. I could see what Maroonie was thinking. Moments later, his strategy was clear to me. I opened my eyes. "Taman and Vensolio. Take your troupes to the back. Make an attack formation," I said. "What? But Why?" Vensolio asked. "Maroonie is going with half of his army to attack us from the back. He wants to sandwich us. We cannot let that happen. They are not going there the right way. They are taking the help of The Book of Destiny to teleport themselves. The moment they arrive, attack!" They nodded and went back.

A few moments later, Maroonie and his troupe disappeared. I knew exactly what was happening. On the back side, Maroonie appeared. He was surprised to find Taman and Vensolio there. A battle raged. Maroonie failed there. In an ongoing battle, he slipped away and rode back to the main battleground. He went back to Lavenred. "You saw what happened, right?" Maroonie asked Lavenred. "Yes. You better do something good this time," Lavenred told him. "But how did Anay come to know? None of us told him. He has no microphones here. Then how?" Maroonie asked. "Did you look into his eyes?" Lavenred asked. Maroonie nodded, confused. "This explains it!" Lavenred said. "This explains it how?" Maroonie asked. "He is a telepath! He can read minds, but only if there is eye contact," Lavenred said. "No eye contact with him!" Maroonie nodded. "What do we to do now? Vensolio has set up a protective shield around his entire army. None of our weapons can penetrate it. We cannot finish him that way. "There is a slight color difference. That is the boundary of their layer. Every couple of minutes, a weak zone appears on the top. The only way to enter is from there. Wait for it to come and launch a missile into it. That should hit Vensolio. It should only weaken him. I don't want him dead," Lavenred said. Maroonie looked at him in awe. "Yes sir!" he said. "You have seven minutes and eighteen seconds. Go prepare your ammunition!" Lavenred said. "Yes sir!" Maroonie said, and left for the arena. He came in and stood at a far end. Sanya noticed him. "Anay!" she said, and pointed her finger towards Maroonie. Taman and Vensolio were back now. A hundred men were killed, but they had finished a major part of the enemy. "What is he up to now?" Sanya asked. "Let me see!" I said. I tried to read what he was thinking, but I was unsuccessful. "He is not making any eye contact with me!" I said. "I am not of much help now."

The battle raged on. We were only half-focusing on what was going on in the battlefield. We observed Maroonie. He took a huge gun-like thing in hand and aimed high in the sky. After a few seconds, he shot a missile into the sky. I had no clue what was happening. Maroonie's smiled a crooked smile. Only then, he made an eye contact with me. I looked into his eyes, and saw what was going to happen. The arrow was about to hit Vensolio! My heart was beating fast, I broke eye contact and screamed, "Vensolio! Look out! A miss!" I was too late. The arrow had hit Vensolio on his right shoulder. He was badly injured. "In ...... in this condition I cannot hold the shield for a long time!" Vensolio said, with agony visible on his face. Sanya took him and sat on the seat, treating his wounds. With each passing second, our shield became weaker and weaker. The enemy attacks where affecting us now. I was watching this all in horror.

Taman came up to me. "If this continues, we will lose! We need to do something," Taman said. I looked at him for a second. "Do you think it is time?" I said, looking right into his eyes. He understood what I was talking about. "The... the Destructive Fireworks Protocol?" Taman asked. I nodded. "If we don't do this now, we won't be able to save our world from the evil deeds of this person. Taman, order the troupes to initiate the Destructive Fireworks Protocol!" I said. He turned around with the speaker and announced: "Troupes! Initiate Destructive Fireworks Protocol!" We stood there with our heads down. "Vensolio!" I said, "Break the shield. Let them leave." Vensolio did so.

Sanya's medicine was helping him. Our troupes left. Maroonie and Lavenred had no idea what was happening. Maroonie was with the rest of the army. Our soldiers set up a perimeter around them. They began edging closer. The enemy's army was contained within our soldiers' perimeter. I looked into Sanya's eyes. She stared at me for a moment and nodded with a tear trickling down her eye. I nodded to our Commander, who was a part of the perimeter. He acknowledged my request. I closed my eyes. There was a huge explosion. Each of our soldiers was a human bomb. We triggered them all. The eruption killed their army. Our soldiers were gone too. The battle field was full of blood and dead bodies. Severed limbs were scattered. Maroonie was dead too. The only ones alive were Vensolio, Taman, Sanya, Lavenred and me. Vensolio was alright now.

Lavenred recovered from the shock fast. He jumped off his tower and entered the arena. The four of us were ready. We entered the arena. Lavenred came walking, with a sword in his hand. "Let's finish this the traditional way," he said.

"Nothing can save you now from your death!" I said. We dismounted from our horses. We ran with our swords in hand. It was Vensolio and me with our swords in hand. Taman and Sanya supported us from behind. A loud clashing sound burst into the silent scene. A dangerous sword fight took place.

Lavenred fought two on one. I gave him a down stroke while Vensolio's strong attack threw him away. He was knocked down. We had our swords on his neck. "Y … You think you've got me?" he said with a sly smile. I was confused. What could he have done? And then it dawned on me. MIND CONTROL! ON VENSOLIO! "Vensolio don't look into his eyes! Venso" I choked as I saw the scene. It was too late. Lavenred had gotten control over Vensolio! "Hey you! Now cast your most dangerous spell on all of them!" Lavenred ordered. Vensolio nodded, and shook his fingers after muttering something. He had made us immortal! How could that curse be used! It was forbidden!

But it already was too late. "You filthy rat!" I ran towards Lavenred with my sword in hand. He struck me and I fell. I was gasping for breath. "Now let's see if immorality can help you survive this stroke!" Lavenred said with his sword held high. He was about to kill me, but something strange happened. Lavenred fell down on me. When he crashed onto me, I saw a sword poking out of his back. We were surprised. "How did that happen?" Vensolio asked. We saw a man standing in front of Anay. Due to darkness, his face was not visible. I look my sword in my hand and stood up. "Now who the hell are you?" I asked. He said nothing, but walked a step forward. Gradually, his face became visible. Our jaws dropped. My heart skipped a beat. "Back from the dead, eh?" I asked with the voice that was left in me. "Come here!" I asked as I dropped the sword and hugged him. He was Vikram. The others joined in. "How did you do this?" Taman asked. "Remember the day I ran away? It was not just an idiot running out of emotional needs. It was my plan to finish Lavenred. It has been my plan ever since. I was never a man sent by Lavenred, Anay. It was all a bluff. The day I met you guys, I knew you won't be able to do such a thing without my dying. But it was all correctly timed. I knew my death would give you a push. So I did what was necessary. I am sorry if any of it hurt you!" Vikram said. We listened as though we were five-year-old kids listening to a story teller.

"But … but what about those visions?" It clearly said you would die. Why did I not get the complete scene?" I asked. Vikram smiled disarmingly.

"Your visions," Vikram said, "are another secret."

"What?"

"Yes, you heard right."

"Well, then tell me about it."

"You are not ready for it."

"What do you mean by that?"

"With time, my friend, you will get all your answers!" Vikram said, and walked past me. I was surprised.

"Shall we leave?" Vikram asked. "Yes. It's time we do so," Vensolio said. "Okay then." I picked up the book, and wrote in it. "Take five of us back to the Earth" and read it aloud. Just when we were transported, I threw the book back. On our way, I saw two things: Lavenred and the Book of Destiny. With that vision, I retired to the Earth.

limbs of the guards. A boy ran into our cabin and Vensolio altered the wall by magic.

"Now, who are you?" Vensolio asked exasperated, "Is this the way to enter?" "Hey boy! Calm down! I am Alkazar!" he said in his strong but strange voice. Taman and Vensolio looked at him strangely.

"Alkazar? What kind of a name is that? From day one I am facing weird names and ..." Taman said, and I cut him off.

"He is just like us!" I said.

"What?" both of them asked.

"He lost his parents, too. They were also killed by Lavenred. Alkazar has sworn revenge," I said.

"Yes! How do you know?" he asked. "It happened to us, too. We want to kill the rogue!" Taman said, exasperated.

"I don't think you can do this alone. Will you join us?" I asked him with hope.

"Yes!" he said, joyfully. We had an expert in chemistry and physics with us, now. Alkazar mingled with us. He was jolly, and a good friend. There was only one person left. Who was it? When will luck introduce us to him? Fire had set in, only wind was left. A wind which would groom this fire into something big enough to eat up the entire forest. The fifth shadow changed history.

Chapter 13

Sanya

It was a normal day in prison. We sat together in Vensolio's cabin. We had breakfast. We always told Vensolio to make us food with magic. Each time it was a different delicacy. Food was always awesome, for breakfast, lunch and dinner. One night, we had too much noodles for dinner. We burped continuously. "Delicious! What food!" said Alkazar, licking his fingers. The others nodded in agreement.

"We must find a way to defeat Lavenred. He is growing more powerful by the day," I said.

"Yes, I agree with you!" Taman said.

"Me too!" said Vensolio.

"What will I do here alone? I am with you too!" Alkazar said. We started discussing it more seriously. Everyone shared their best ideas. Some were powerful, some were useless, but all ideas were useful.

YEAR 2034, A PARTICULAR NIGHT

I slept normally. Suddenly, I felt a jerk in my head. I opened my eyes and looked around. I was in a dream. I could hear footsteps. Gradually, the figure of a man appeared. He was my dad. "Where have you been, dad? We won!" I said, excited. Dad smiled. I was flummoxed. "Are you not happy with this victory?" I asked.

"Victory? This is not a victory, son! It's a milestone indicating that you now are a step closer to Victory," Dad said in calmness and serenity.
"What do you mean? I don't get it!" I said. "Do you think that the purpose of your existence is fulfilled? No, son! You are destined to do something big, something huge. Today it was Lavenred, and the Book of Destiny. But the Ocean of Evil is deeper than what you think. Tomorrow there will be a greater power, and some person who is more evil. They will have to be defeated. That, my son, will be your and your friend's true need. You will re-unite to defeat them," Dad said.

"Why only us? Whom will we defeat? And when do we meet again?" I asked.

"With time, you will get answers," he said as he began walking away. I descended into sleep again. I could hear dad saying one thing "And you will unite … Because the world will need you to!"

The End